# The Girl in the

Written by Narinder Dhami

Illustrated by Wendy Leach

## Collins

# 1 The girl opposite

Rajni lived at the top of a block of flats in the city of Mumbai in India. She loved living so high up in the clouds. It was almost like flying! She could see all the tiny people below, running around like ants. But most of all, Rajni liked to wave to her friend who lived in the flat opposite.

Rajni didn't know her friend's name because they'd never met. But she knew they'd be best friends if they ever got to know each other. Her friend lived with her parents, and no one else. Rajni thought the flat opposite always looked tidy and peaceful. *Her* home was very different!

Sheela didn't know the name of the girl who lived opposite because they'd never met. She was sure they'd be best friends if they ever did meet, though. Sheela could see that her friend lived with her parents, her four brothers and sisters, her gran and a white cat.

Sheela had been ill for a few months and was waiting for an operation. Sometimes she felt very tired, so her parents liked her to be quiet and rest. Sheela enjoyed having her own bedroom and plenty of space to play. But she thought Rajni was lucky to have so much fun with her brothers and sisters.

Rajni loved her loud, lively family, but she often wished she lived in her friend's quiet flat. Sometimes she could hardly think properly when she was doing her homework. And her little brother Ricky was the biggest pest of all time! He was *always* annoying her!

Sheela couldn't go to school until she was well again. So, she had a home tutor instead. Sheela liked her tutor and enjoyed her lessons, but she missed seeing her friends. Every morning, she watched Rajni leave for school in her smart clothes. Her friend had a purple school bag and a lunchbox with rainbows on it.

*I wish I could go to school!* Sheela thought enviously.

Rajni sometimes watched Sheela painting pictures, reading a book or playing computer games. Her friend didn't have to share a bedroom with anyone. She had lots of toys and games, and her own computer. She didn't even have to go to school.

*She's so lucky!* Rajni thought enviously. Sheela seemed to have so much more freedom than she did.

## 2 Hide-and-seek!

The two girls knew a lot about each other's lives. Sheela had worked out that Rajni's dad travelled abroad for his job, and when he arrived home the family always had a special meal.

Rajni had been very envious when she saw a brand-new TV appear in Sheela's bedroom. She didn't think she'd ever be allowed her own TV.

"Come on, Rajni," Mum called one morning.
"We're going to see Auntie Neela." Auntie Neela lived downstairs in a ground-floor flat.

"Can I go to the playground?" Ricky asked eagerly.

"If you're a good boy," Mum replied. "Rajni can look after you."

"Oh, *Mum*!" Rajni groaned. "Last time, he dug a hole in the sandpit and buried my book!"

Sheela was watching from the opposite window as
Rajni, Ricky and their mum prepared to go out.
Rajni had a book tucked under her arm, and Ricky was
wearing his favourite lime-green trainers, the ones with
the flashing lights around the soles. Rajni was pulling
a face at Ricky, and he was laughing.

*They always have so much fun together,* Sheela thought.
*I wish I had a little brother just like him!*

"Can we play hide-and-seek in the playground?" Ricky begged Rajni.

"We *always* play hide-and-seek!" Rajni groaned. "Why don't you play football with your friends?"

Ricky was annoyed. "You just want to read your silly book!" he muttered.

"Now, you two behave yourselves," Mum warned them. "I'll be watching you from Auntie Neela's window."

Ricky rushed off ahead, and Rajni had to grab
his hand. The playground was part of the estate,
and only the children who lived in the apartment
blocks were allowed to play there. Rajni knew everyone,
although she'd never seen her friend from the opposite
flat in the playground.

"*Can* we play hide-and-seek?" Ricky demanded.

"I'd rather read my book," Rajni muttered. She'd just reached an exciting part of the story, and she was longing to know what happened next.

"Hide-and-seek!" Ricky roared at full volume. "Or I'll tell Mum you secretly scoffed all the samosas!"

"All right!" Rajni agreed.

"I've thought of a *brilliant* new hiding place," Ricky replied gleefully. "You'll never find me."

"You hide first," Rajni sighed. She covered her eyes with her hands and began to count. "One, two, three ..."

"Make sure you count to 100!" Ricky warned her.

## 3 Under the tunnel

Ricky went over to the tunnels in
the middle of the playground. The tunnels
were made of brightly-coloured plastic,
and they all linked up with each other.
There was a gap between the tunnels
and the ground. It was the perfect
hiding place!

Ricky waved at his mum, who was
watching him from Auntie Neela's window.
Then he laid down on his tummy
and slid underneath the blue tunnel.
Purring, Bella followed him.

"Rajni won't find us here," Ricky told Bella. "This is the best hiding place ever!"

Bella yawned, curled into a ball and went to sleep.

*I bet Rajni gives up, and I win!* Ricky thought gleefully. *I wonder if she's counted to 100 yet?*

But Rajni had stopped counting when she got to 32. Smiling to herself, she sat down on a nearby bench and opened her book. At last, she had some peace and quiet to read her story. Wherever Ricky and Bella were hiding, they could stay there until she'd finished her book!

Rajni read for a long time. Meanwhile, Ricky was getting impatient. Where *was* his sister? She could easily have counted to *500* by this time!

At last, Rajni closed her book. It would be easy to find Ricky because he always hid in the same places. Then she remembered Ricky had said he'd discovered a new hiding place. Well, it wouldn't take her long to find him!

Underneath the tunnel, Ricky saw his sister's pink trainers hurry past him. He clapped a hand over his mouth to stop himself bursting out laughing. Rajni hadn't noticed him!

Sheela was up in her flat. She was supposed to be doing her homework, but instead she'd borrowed her dad's binoculars. Sheela watched the other children enjoying themselves and wished she was well enough to join in. She'd seen her friend sitting on the bench reading her book. But now her friend had finished reading and was walking around the playground.

But what was *that* sticking out from underneath the blue tunnel?

Sheela stared through the binoculars. She was amazed to see a lime-green trainer poking out from underneath the blue tunnel. The trainer had flashing lights around the sole.

"It's my friend's brother!" Sheela gasped. "But why is he lying so still? He must be injured!"

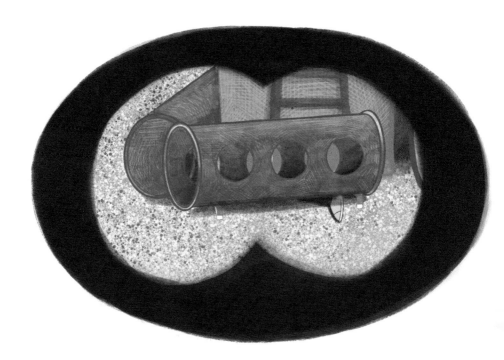

Through the binoculars, Sheela saw her friend running around the playground, searching for her brother.

"He's underneath the tunnel!" Sheela shouted. But, of course, Rajni couldn't hear her from so high up.

## 4 Where's Ricky?

Rajni couldn't understand it. She'd searched all around the playground twice and checked every single place she could think of. Ricky wasn't anywhere to be found, and there was nowhere else left to look.

Then she noticed some of Ricky's friends playing football. Rajni sprinted over immediately to ask them if they'd seen her brother. But none of them had.

Sheela dashed into the kitchen. Her mum was frying garlic and ginger to make curry, and her dad was ironing his kurta pyjamas.

"My friend's brother is injured!" Sheela cried. "We have to help him!"

Sheela's parents didn't understand at first until Sheela gave them the binoculars to see for themselves. Ricky was still lying under the tunnel.

"Please can we go and see if he's all right?" Sheela asked.

"Oh dear," Sheela's mum said anxiously. "I don't want you to go outside, Sheela. There's a cold wind today."

"Please, Mum!" Sheela begged. "I'll wear my coat and scarf."

"All right," her mum agreed. "Put your gloves on, too."

*Where can Ricky be?* Rajni wondered. She didn't know
where to search next, and she was beginning
to panic. *I wish I hadn't read my book for such a long time,*
she thought. *This is all my fault. Ricky could
be anywhere!*

Rajni glanced at her mum who waved at her from Auntie Neela's window. Rajni realised that Mum didn't look worried at all. Perhaps Ricky had discovered such a brilliant hiding place, that Rajni couldn't find him? Or maybe Ricky had wandered off on his own, and Mum hadn't noticed? Rajni suddenly felt very cold inside.

"I give up, Ricky!" Rajni shouted. "You win! You'd better come out now."

Ricky grinned triumphantly to himself. He was about to crawl out from under the tunnel when he hesitated. This was his favourite hiding place *ever*.

*If Rajni doesn't find out where I'm hiding,* Ricky thought, *then I can hide in the same place next time!*

So Ricky decided to remain where he was. As soon as Rajni had gone somewhere else, then he'd come out. Rajni would never know he'd been underneath the blue tunnel!

# 5 Sheela to the rescue!

Sheela rushed to grab her scarf and coat. There was no time to waste! She was desperate to get down to the playground and help her friend to find her brother. She hoped he wasn't badly injured, but he was lying so very still and quiet.

Sheela and her mum hurried into the lift. It seemed to take ages to travel down to the ground floor. Sheela hopped impatiently from one foot to the other, wishing it would go faster.

The playground was crowded with children and their parents. They all lived in the flats on the estate, but Sheela didn't know any of them. She was hardly ever allowed to go to the playground. The children stared curiously at Sheela as she rushed past them with her mum. Most of them didn't recognise her, and they had no idea she lived in the flats.

"Who's she?" the children whispered to each other.

Sheela blushed. She felt uncomfortable because everyone was staring at her. But she was determined to find out if her friend's brother was hurt or not. Maybe they'd have to call an ambulance.

"There he is, Mum!" Sheela gasped, when they reached the blue tunnel. "Look, he still hasn't moved."

"Is he all right?" her mum asked.

Sheela bent down and touched the flashing, lime-green trainer.

Ricky gave a yelp, and Sheela jumped backwards in surprise.

"Who are you, and why are you grabbing my foot?" Ricky asked indignantly. He tried to wriggle out from under the tunnel, but it was a tight fit. Sheela grabbed his arm and helped him squeeze out.

"I'm Sheela, and I thought you were hurt," Sheela explained.

"I'm Ricky, and I'm fine!" Ricky grumbled. "I'm playing hide-and-seek with my sister Rajni."

*Rajni?* Sheela thought, with a smile. *So that's my friend's name! It's pretty.*

"You're very little to be out on your own," Sheela's mum remarked.

"I'm *not* little," Ricky said crossly. "I'm five! Look, there's my mum." He pointed to his mother sitting in Auntie Neela's window. Sheela's mum hurried over to say hello.

"Rajni's searching everywhere for you, Ricky," Sheela told him. "She's really worried."

"Is she?" Ricky grinned. "Rajni says I'm a pest sometimes!"

Sheela laughed. She wished she had a cheeky little brother like Ricky and a fluffy cat like Bella. Rajni was so lucky!

# 6 Where's Rajni?

Rajni's heart was thumping, and she was struggling not to cry. She'd crossed the football field to the tall gates that were always kept locked. Maybe Bella had jumped over the high walls, and Ricky had gone after her? He might be small enough to squeeze through the bars of the gate.

The street outside the estate was busy with traffic streaming along very fast. It was a dangerous road. Miserably, Rajni peered through the bars of the gate. But there was no sign of Ricky or Bella.

"We ought to go and find Rajni," Sheela told Ricky.

"No, she has to come and find *me* because we're playing hide-and-seek!" Ricky laughed. "Do you like spiders?" And he pulled a big fake spider out of his pocket. Sheela grinned.

"Rajni hates spiders," Ricky said, his eyes twinkling with mischief. "She tells me off when I tease her."

"Oh!" Sheela said, surprised. She'd thought Rajni liked Ricky's jokes.

"And she says I'm too noisy," Ricky added.
Secretly, Sheela thought that Rajni was right.
Ricky *was* quite loud!

Suddenly, Ricky bent down and grabbed a green ball that was rolling towards him. He threw the ball at Sheela who caught it neatly, and then he ran off behind the tunnels out of sight.

A tall girl raced across the playground towards Sheela. "Why have you got my ball?" she demanded.
She didn't look very friendly.

"Sorry," Sheela said, embarrassed.

The girl grabbed the ball and ran off. Ricky appeared from behind the tunnels, bent over double with laughter.

"Did you know that ball was hers, Ricky?" Sheela asked a little crossly.

"Of course I knew it was Meera's ball!" Ricky chuckled.

"Do you always play tricks on people?" Sheela asked curiously.

"Yes," Ricky replied, with a cheeky grin. "Sorry." He pulled a bag of sweets from his pocket and offered them to Sheela.

"Thank you," Sheela said, popping one into her mouth. As she sucked the sweet, it suddenly tasted very hot and peppery. Coughing, Sheela threw the sweet in the bin.

"They're joke sweets!" Ricky chuckled.

Sheela sighed. Ricky was cute and she liked him, but it would be very annoying if he played tricks all the time. Maybe having a little brother *wasn't* always fun!

"What's Bella doing?" Sheela asked.

"Oh, she likes to chase birds," Ricky replied.
"And mice, too. Bella's naughty! She's always climbing up the curtains, and she loves shredding paper everywhere."

Sheela's eyes opened wide. She hadn't realised that pets could be such hard work!

# 7 Friends forever

By now, Rajni was very frightened. She knew she'd have to go and confess to her mum that she'd read her book instead of playing with Ricky.

*What if I never see Ricky again?* Rajni wondered. She gulped, trying not to cry. Ricky *was* a pest sometimes, but they did have fun together.

41

Rajni trudged miserably back to the playground.
She knew she was going to be in a lot of trouble.
But who was that boy standing by the tunnels with
a cat in his arms? Rajni could hardly believe her eyes.
It was Ricky and Bella!

Overjoyed, Rajni raced over and grabbed Ricky and
Bella in a bear hug.

"Stop it!" Ricky yelped, wriggling away from her.
"Look, this is Sheela. She lives opposite us."

"I know," Rajni said, with a grin.
"We're already friends!"

Rajni and Sheela stared at each other.

"We're the same height," Rajni said. "I thought you were taller."

"I thought *you* were taller!" Sheela laughed.

"I'm really jealous of you!" Rajni told her. "Your flat is so tidy and quiet. And you have your own bedroom and loads of stuff to play with."

"I like having my own room," Sheela replied. "But you're so lucky to have brothers and sisters and a pet."

The girls looked at each other in surprise.

"I wish I could go to school, like you," Sheela said longingly. "But I'm not well enough."

"You're sick?" Rajni asked, shocked.

Sheela nodded. "I'm waiting for an operation, and then I'll be fine," she replied. "But I get lonely at home because I can't go out much."

Rajni thought for a moment. She was *never* lonely. There was always someone at home to talk to. Rajni had lots of friends at school, too.

43

"Maybe it's a good thing you haven't got a little brother like Ricky, if you're ill," Rajni said, with a grin. "You'd never get any peace and quiet!"

"I know," Sheela agreed. "He's cute, and so is Bella, but I think they'd tire me out very quickly!"

"Maybe we can ask our mums if we can visit each other," Rajni suggested. "Then you can come and play with me, Ricky and Bella whenever you feel well enough."

"And you can visit *me* and get some peace and quiet whenever you want!" Sheela added, with a smile.

"Ricky and Bella are in the sandpit," Sheela said, pointing across the playground. "Look, they're digging a hole together."

Rajni noticed that her book had gone from the bench. "They're burying my book again!" she gasped.

Laughing, Rajni and Sheela hurried across the playground together. Now, at last, they would get to know each other properly and become *real* friends!

# Diaries

## Sheela's diary:

This is a really SPECIAL day! I met my friend Rajni for the first time, and we talked for ages. I thought I knew all about her and her family, but I found out that not everything was what it seemed. I used to wish I had a big family and a pet like Rajni does, but now I understand why my parents like me to stay quietly at home. Ricky and Bella are cute, but they'd wear me out in five minutes! I like being quieter sometimes.

## Rajni's diary:

When I woke up this morning, I never dreamt that today would be so amazing. I've finally met my friend Sheela who lives opposite me, and we felt like best friends straightaway! I didn't realise Sheela was ill, though. That's why she stays at home and doesn't go to school. I used to envy her a lot, but now I think she's very brave. It'll be great to go and visit her, though, to get away from Ricky's jokes!

#  Ideas for reading

## Written by Clare Dowdall, PhD
### Lecturer and Primary Literacy Consultant

**Reading objectives:**
- discuss and clarify the meanings of words, linking new meanings to known vocabulary
- make inferences on the basis of what is being said and done
- predict what might happen on the basis of what has been read so far

**Spoken language objectives:**
- give well-structured descriptions and explanations

- use spoken language to develop understanding through speculating, hypothesising, imagining and exploring ideas

**Curriculum links:** PSHE – relationships

**Word count:** 2992

**Interest words:** opposite, enviously, jealous, samosas

**Resources:** art materials for drawing a view from a window, whiteboards, pencils and paper

## Build a context for reading

- Ask children to describe how it feels when they make new friends.

- Look at the front cover and ask children to describe what they can see and to suggest what is happening.

- Read the blurb together. Discuss why they think the girls in the story haven't been able to meet properly, and what "meeting properly" means.

## Understand and apply reading strategies

- Ask children to read Chapter 1 as a group. Discuss what the chapter title *The girl opposite* means.

- Help children to notice how the story is structured and told from two different perspectives, and through two windows. Ask children to explain why the two girls are envious of each other, and help them to make inferences about how they feel at this stage in the story. Check that children understand the meaning of the word *envious*.